The Moon's
Almost
Here

For Lucy, with love, Ama
—P. M.

For Sherry, my art buddy
—T. deP.

The Moon's Almost Here

Patricia MacLachlan

ILLUSTRATED BY

Tomie dePaola

Margaret K. McElderry Books
New York   London   Toronto   Sydney   New Delhi

The moon's almost here!
Robin sings in her nest.
Babies fly back to her,
Ready to rest.

The moon's almost here.
There's no time to play.
Mama sheep hurries;
Sun's going away.

"The moon's almost here,"
Clucks plump mother hen.
Chicks settle under her,
Safe in their pen.

The moon's almost here.
Mama duck drifts to shore.
Ducklings swim after:
One, two, three, and four.

The moon's almost here.
Mare whinnies a song.
Cow moos to her calves
And they follow along.

The moon's almost here.
The butterfly knows.
She sits on a flower,

Then—
Quickly she goes.

Out in the meadow
The fireflies blink bright.

Twinkling on,
Twinkling off—
Little stars in the night.

Sweet dog on the porch
Can see the moon rise.

He curls in a ball
And closes his eyes.

Good night little dog,
Dreams in your head.

Good night little kitten,
Warm in my bed.

Good night fireflies,
Lighting my night.

Welcome white moon,

So big